My M

and I
A Covid Story

Jane Dugbo

Illustrated by
Tara Warden

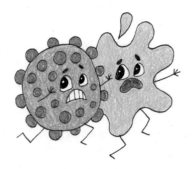

ISBN: 9798598115305

To my husband who has always been my best support and truth-teller. You ARE the only person who will give it to me straight.

To my daughter who has spent hours making sure this book was perfect! That's my girl!

To my son who is my go-to-guru for anything techie. You can thank him for my great website.

Lastly, to all of you who are wanting to do the right thing by trying to social distance, self-quarantine, wash, wash, wash your hands for that interminable 20 seconds, and finally to wear a mask that affects your freedom of breathing.

You Rock! Your sacrifice is appreciated.

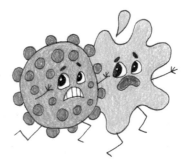

I live by my mask and
Will forever continue
Till Covid is gone
And we have a new menu

But until then, my friend
My mask will be on

In my bed

And my bath

In my garden with the birds

In my chair with the cat

With my friends
At my school
While looking
So cool

Or Zooming online

Until the teacher says,"Time!"

No cough, no sneeze
Will get me sick 'cause
I wear a mask and
I give it a kick

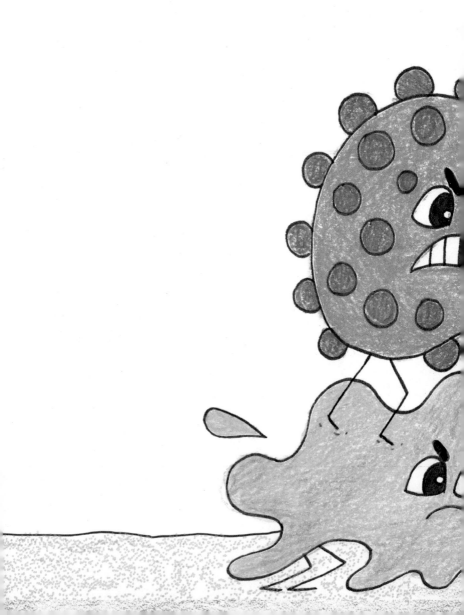

My mask, my friend, is close to me

So as you can see
No sneeze, no cough
Can ever reach me

I'm wearing one with a mouse

I'm wearing one on a plane

I'm wearing one on a train

I will wear one
In the car
I will wear one
Near and far

I will wear my mask
When I'm up at dawn

I will wear my mask
Until Covid is through
I will clean my mask
Using bubbly shampoo

ICE CREAM

vanilla . . . .
Chocolate . . . . .
Strawberry . . . .
Cookies n'cream
mint chocolate c
Buttered pecan
moose tracks . .

I will wear
My mask
While at
The store

I will wear my mask
In front of the door

No sneeze no cough will fly by me
No way, I say
No way!

The mask, my friend,
Is my shield and guard
To take care of you
And take care of **Bernard**
And all of those who will
Heed the call
To stop this madness and
Stop this great fall

Let's give Covid a kick

And give Covid a shove

So we can come home
To give a great hug

To our loved ones, our neighbors
Our friends and our dog

Our storekeepers, farmers...

Or even
A hog

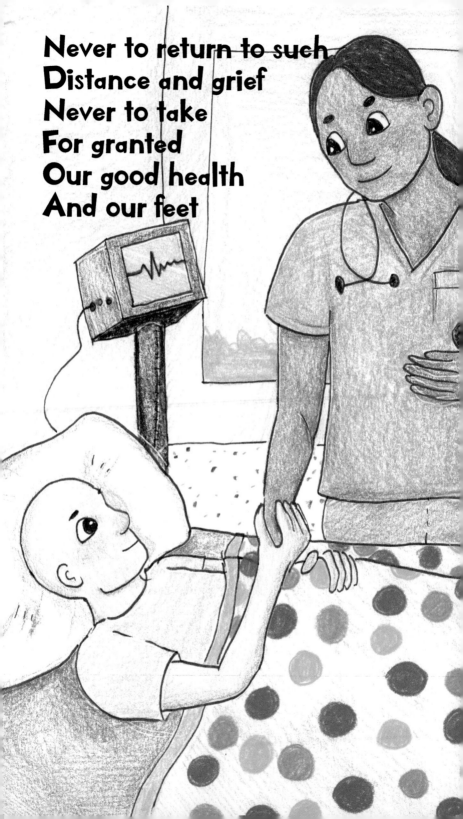

Never to return to such
Distance and grief
Never to take
For granted
Our good health
And our feet

So we can visit the poor
And lift up the downtrodden
To give of ourselves and
Take care
Of the fallen

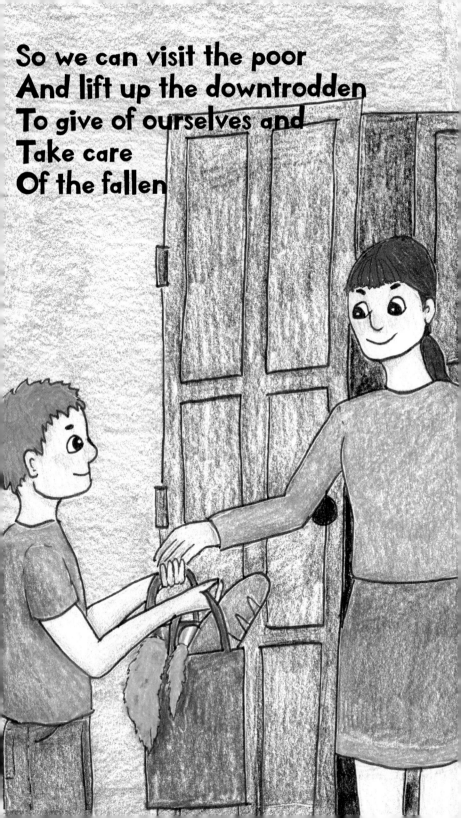

I will win, you shall see
We'll all live to be free

With a mask and a plan
To live high and live well

How can we lose?
Who can we tell?

As I live by my mask
And live to be free
6ft away I dare it to flee
For Covid won't be here in 2023

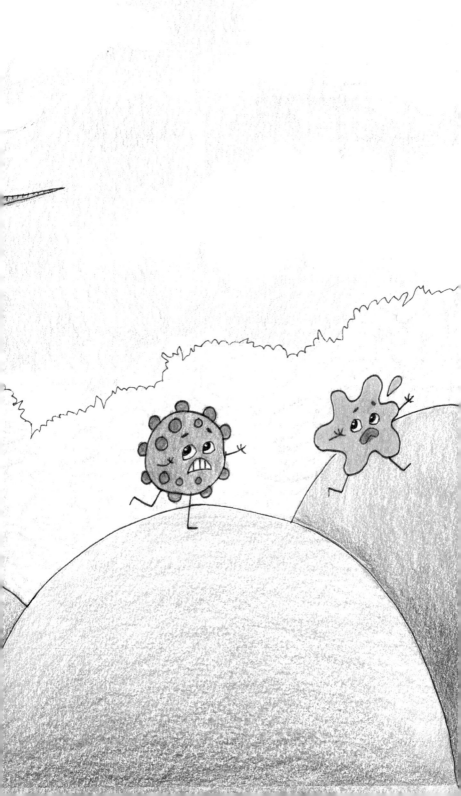

This sneeze and this cough
Will not have a say
As we wear our masks proudly
And step out of the way

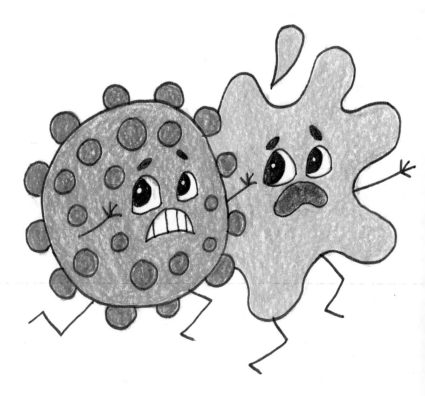

Until Covid is gone
Let's all get along
Be polite and unite
And fight the good fight

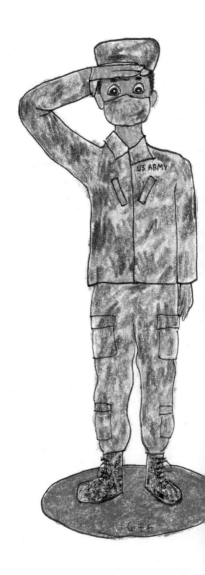

Such a story to say
Such a story to tell

Let's all wear our masks
And be done

And live
Well

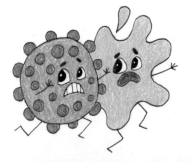

About The Author

Jane Head Dugbo is a Marriage and Family Therapist and new author. Being in lockdown during the Covid Pandemic has provided her with an opportunity to step into the world of writing. Understanding that change is stressful, Jane was inspired to encourage kids and parents alike to find a way to cope with the uncertainty and anxiety of our ever changing world through this book.

About The Illustrator

Tara Warden currently is an art student working on her fine art degree at John Brown University.
She loves trying new things. All of her artistic endeavors can be found on her Instagram, @tara.cuda

Made in the USA
Monee, IL
24 February 2021